I SCREAM, ICE CREAM!

Indeed, those are phonetically identical phrases. Who made this book, anyway?

Amy Krouse Rosenthal & Serge Bloch!

oh, and these guys, too:

chronicle books · san francisco

I scream! Two bucks!

Ice cream, two bucks!

Rain, dear.

Me, cloud.

Meek.

Loud.

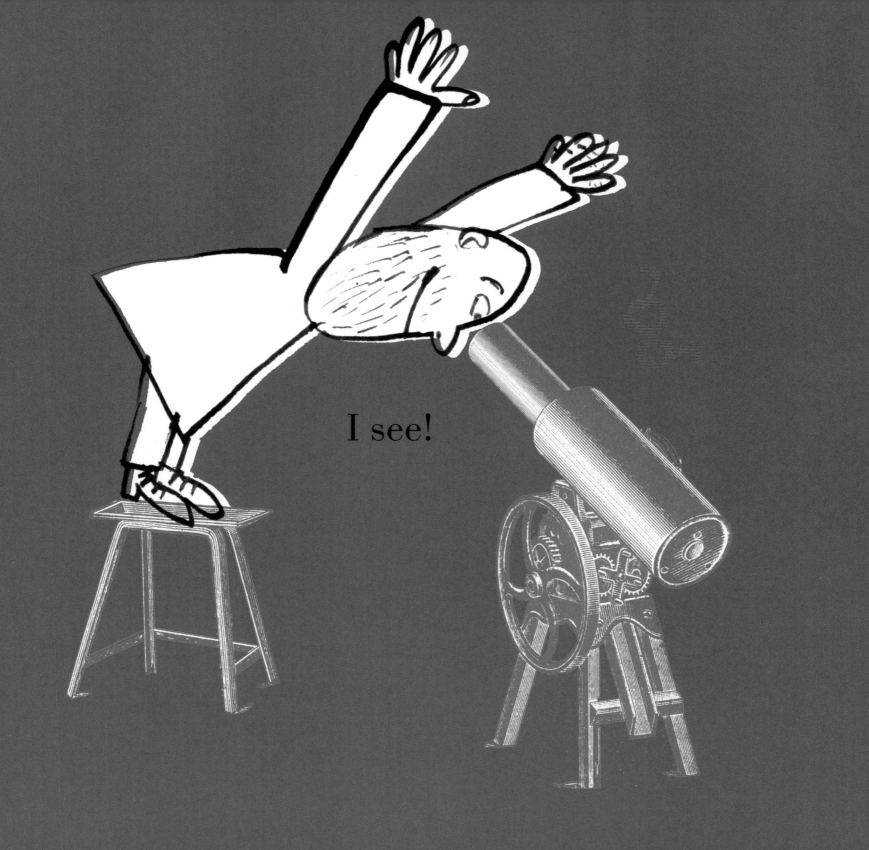

I see!

Pant . . . sneeze.

Sorry, no more funnel cakes.

Sorry, no more fun . . .
elk aches.

WHO DID IT?

Uh, not her.

A knotter?

An otter!

Princess cape.

Clothes!
The wind!
Oh!

An apple . . . doom me good.

A family affair.

A family of hair.

Peace mitten.

Pea smitten.

Thank you to the wonderful students at
the International School of Bangkok who
suggested the Snow White setting for the
A nap'll/An apple wordle. (Can you guess
the other possible setting?) —A. K. R.

Library of Congress Cataloging-
in-Publication Data available.
ISBN 978-1-4521-0004-3

Book design by Sara Gillingham Studio.
Typeset in Bodoni and HandMade OT.

Manufactured in China.

MIX
Paper from
responsible sources
FSC
www.fsc.org   FSC® C008047

10 9 8 7 6 5 4 3 2 1

Chronicle Books LLC
680 Second Street
San Francisco, California 94107

www.chroniclekids.com